Recipe for Disaster

By Remy as told to Laura Driscoll
Illustrated by Caroline LaVelle Egan

Chapter 1

I should have been in rat heaven. And if I were any other rat, I would have been. But I had to make things difficult. There I was, with my rat colony, sitting on a compost heap, surrounded by a huge pile of rotting food. The other rats loved eating this stuff. But I felt we could do better. I should introduce myself. My name's Remy. I'm just your average rat. Except for one thing—I have highly developed senses of taste and smell. Even for a rat.

I found a piece of pastry in the heap and sniffed it. "Flour, eggs, sugar, vanilla bean . . ." Now, this was worth eating.

Disney · PIXAR
RATATOUILLE
(rat·a·too·ee)

Recipe for Disaster

A STEPPING STONE BOOK™

Random House 🏠 New York

Library of Congress Control Number: 2006939389

ISBN: 978-0-7364-2449-3

www.randomhouse.com/kids/disney

Printed in the United States of America

10 9 8 7 6 5 4 3 2 1   First Edition

My big brother Emile looked up. "You can smell all that?" he said. "You have a gift."

Emile was easily impressed. My dad, Django, wasn't. Dad was the leader of our colony. He thought my "gift" was pretty useless—until we both realized I could smell rat poison. Then Dad gave me a job as "poison checker." From then on, I sniffed every bit of food the colony collected. I know. Dull, right?

Yeah, well, it made my dad proud.

"You've helped a noble cause," he told me as I sniffed the millionth scrap of the day.

"Noble?" I repeated. "We're thieves, Dad." I hated that we took these scraps.

"It isn't stealing if no one wants it," Dad argued.

Let's just say we had different points of view. This much I know: if you are what you eat, then I only wanted to eat the good stuff.

I guess that was why I did what I did. See, our rat colony lived in the attic of a cottage.

Dad always said to stay away from the humans. But I couldn't help myself; I had to try some real food. One night, I snuck into the kitchen. Mabel, the old woman who lived in the cottage, was napping in front of the TV.

I scurried onto the counter. There, next to the stove, was a cookbook called *Anyone Can Cook!* On the cover was a picture of the man who was on TV right then: Chef Auguste Gusteau. "Good food is like music you can taste, color you can smell," he said.

I listened closely—until a lamp switched on. The old woman had woken up! I scurried out the window before she could see me.

After that night, I had a secret life. Emile was the only one who knew about it. I went back to the kitchen over and over to read from Gusteau's cookbook. I wanted to try creating something myself!

One day, I began walking on two legs instead of four. Emile thought it was weird, but

I had to keep my paws clean if I was going to work with food. I gathered the perfect ingredients: a fresh mushroom and some gourmet cheese. Emile and I carried everything up to the cottage roof.

I ran up to the smoking chimney and began to cook. I could tell that the food was going to be delicious. But the sky was starting to get dark. It looked like a storm was coming, and Emile was getting nervous.

Lightning flashed and thunder rumbled. Then—*crrrack!*—a bolt of lightning struck the rod we were using to cook the mushroom! The next thing I knew, Emile and I were lying on the ground. Don't worry: we were fine—though a little toasty.

And the food? It smelled amazing. The mushroom was smoky; the cheese was melted. The taste was even better. A pinch of saffron would make it unbelievable. And I knew just where to find it.

Remy learned about saffron in my book, *Anyone Can Cook!* Did he mention that it was a bestseller?

Minutes later, Emile and I were in the kitchen of the cottage. I searched through the spices while he watched the old woman, who was asleep in front of the TV again.

I found a bottle of saffron as Gusteau appeared on the screen. "Great cooking is not for the faint of heart," he was saying. I moved toward the television, hanging on his every word. Emile watched nervously from the kitchen. "Anyone can cook," Gusteau said, "but only the fearless can be great."

I marveled at the poetry of his words. Then the show's host came back on. "Gusteau's restaurant lost one of its five stars after a scathing review by France's top food critic, Anton Ego," he said. "It was a severe blow to Gusteau, and the great chef died shortly afterward, some say of a broken heart."

My knees went weak. I felt light-headed. I didn't want to believe what I was hearing. "Gusteau . . . is dead?" I mumbled, stunned.

Just then, the TV clicked off. In the now dark screen, I saw my reflection and, behind mine, the old woman. She had woken up—and she was staring right at me!

Chapter 2

The old woman came after Emile and me immediately. She didn't seem to care if she ruined her house in the process. When all was said and done, she'd made a huge hole in the ceiling.

A chunk of the attic floor where the rest of the colony lived came crashing down. Rats were everywhere. The colony had been discovered, and now everyone was in danger.

"Evacuate!" shouted Dad. "To the boats!"

The whole colony ran out of the house, toward the river. I wanted to leave, too. But first I had to get Gusteau's cookbook. Cooking was the one thing that made sense to me.

The book was quite heavy, so I was the last one to the river. By the time I got there, the others had already piled into makeshift boats and shoved off. I tossed the cookbook into the water, hopped on, and paddled frantically.

"Remy! You can make it!" I heard my dad shout. But his boat was too far ahead of me. I couldn't catch up. A minute later, I heard rats screaming.

"Dad?" I called, waiting and hoping. "Dad?" I yelled again, a little more desperately. But the tunnel was silent. My heart fell. Then I heard something. The noise was faint at first, and it seemed to be coming from up ahead. Slowly, it grew louder, until . . .

I saw it—a huge waterfall!

The next thing I knew, I was tumbling into the cold, watery darkness.

When I finally stopped floating, I had no idea where I was. I just got out of the water and pulled the cookbook out.

I was cold. I was wet. I couldn't find my family. And as it turned out, I was in a sewer. I flipped through the cookbook, trying to dry the pages. That was when one of the pictures of Gusteau seemed to come to life.

"Go up and look around, Remy," it said. "Why do you wait and mope?"

"I've just lost my family," I replied. "All my friends. Probably forever."

"How do you know?" asked the Gusteau in the book.

It inspires, it talks, and it floats? This cookbook is a steal at twice the price!

"Well, I . . ." Maybe the stink of the sewer was getting to me.

Was I really talking to a cookbook? "You are an illustration. Why am I talking to you?"

Gusteau shrugged. "You are lonely." He smiled. "Now, go up and look around."

So I left the ruined cookbook behind and made my way aboveground. After a long while, I walked onto a rooftop.

All of a sudden, I was looking out over a city twinkling with lights. It was Paris! I had traveled all the way to Paris!

My eyes were drawn to a sign in the distance. It pictured a chef with a familiar face. "Gusteau's?" I said in disbelief.

I had to get a closer look. Within minutes, I was sprawled out on a skylight over his restaurant's kitchen.

Gusteau appeared again. "Let us see how much you know, eh?" he said. He asked me who the people in the kitchen were. I identified them all—the chef, the sous-chef, the cooks—except one, a young man scrubbing a pan.

"Washes dishes or takes out the garbage," I said. "He doesn't cook."

But just then, the garbage boy bumped into a pot, and some soup spilled. He added water and spices to the pot so no one would notice. They were the wrong ingredients.

The boy was completely ruining the soup! "Do something!" I said to Gusteau.

Gusteau shrugged. "What can I do? I am a figment of your imagination."

"But he's ruining the soup!" I screamed.

Suddenly, the skylight window gave way. . . .

I was falling into Gusteau's!

Chapter 3

With a splash, I landed in some dishwater. I had to find a way out. There were humans everywhere! I spotted an open window across the kitchen and ran toward it. Inches from the window, I passed by the soup. I could have made it. But that soup smelled awful.

Gusteau appeared. "You know how to fix it," he said. "This is your chance. . . ."

He was right! I turned the heat down. Then I added new ingredients and water to the pot.

As I was adding some spices, I froze. The garbage boy was watching me, his eyes wide. I guess he'd never seen a rat cook before.

I sprinkled some more spices into the pot just as the chef called for the soup. Then I made a break for the window, but the garbage boy was too fast. He slammed a colander down over me. I was trapped. But at least I was hidden.

"Out of my way!" the chef shouted at the garbage boy. Then he saw a ladle in the boy's hand. "How dare you cook in my kitchen?"

I pushed the colander toward the window as the chef yelled. Meanwhile, a waiter carried the soup out to the dining room . . . and *served it to a famous food critic*!

And guess what? You're gonna love this.

"She liked the soup," the waiter reported.

Someone liked *my* soup! *My* soup! Soup cooked by a rat. The only problem was that everyone thought the garbage boy had made it.

The chef didn't care that the soup had been a hit. He wanted to fire the garbage boy because he was angry that the boy had cooked in the first place.

But a lady cook objected. "How can we claim to represent the name of Gusteau if we don't uphold his most cherished belief?" she asked the chef.

"And what belief is that, Mademoiselle Tatou?" he replied.

"Anyone can cook," she said.

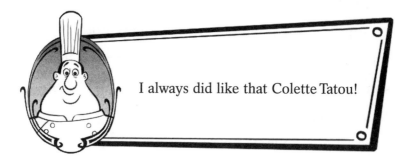

I always did like that Colette Tatou!

As I moved toward the window, I overheard the other cooks agreeing with the lady. Skinner told Linguini he could keep his job, but he'd have to make the soup again.

"They think you might be a cook," the chef told the boy. "I think you are a sneaky, overreaching little—*rat! Raaaat!*"

You might have guessed this, but that was when he spotted yours truly. I raced for the window, but the chef was chasing me with a mop. Before I knew it, he had me cornered.

"Linguini!" the chef yelled at the garbage boy. "Get something to trap it!"

Seconds later, I was inside a glass jar and Linguini had been ordered to take me away—far away—and dispose of me.

I did not like the sound of that.

Chapter 4

Linguini held the jar over the river. I shut my eyes tight and waited for splashdown. After I'd lost my family and friends, after I'd made it to Paris and proven that I could cook, this was how it was going to end?

"Don't look at me like that!" Linguini said suddenly. "You aren't the only one who's trapped. They expect me to cook it again!"

He sat down on the riverbank and put the jar beside him.

"What did you throw in there?" he asked me. "Oregano?"

I shook my head.

"No? What, rosemary?" he asked. "That's a spice, isn't it?"

I couldn't help feeling sorry for him. He looked so . . . defeated. Not to mention he didn't even know what rosemary was. There really was no way he'd be able to make that soup again.

"I need this job," he explained. "I've lost so many. I don't know how to cook and now I'm actually talking to a rat as if you—" He stopped. "You understand me?"

I nodded.

"So I'm not crazy?" he asked. I shook my head. (To be honest, I wasn't really sure about that yet.)

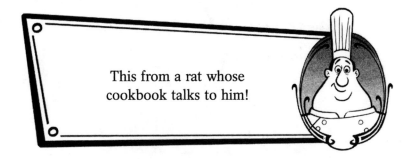

This from a rat whose cookbook talks to him!

"Wait a second. I can't cook. Can I?"

Um, hello, you don't even know what rosemary is. I shook my head.

"But you . . . you can," he said. "Right?"

Just then, Linguini accidentally knocked the jar into the river. But he dove in and pulled me out of the water. After that, I figured he probably wouldn't hurt me.

"They liked the soup," Linguini said. "Do you think you could . . . do it again?"

I nodded.

"I'm going to let you out now," Linguini said. "But we're together on this, right?"

I nodded again. I'd have agreed to anything to get out of that jar.

So Linguini set the jar down and opened it. You know what I did? I made a break for it. I ran as fast as my little legs could carry me. I looked back to make sure I was in the clear.

Linguini hadn't moved from his spot. He just sat there, looking so sad, so alone.

I felt guilty. I slowed down and turned around. I could have kicked myself for being such a pushover. But I couldn't help it. This guy needed me.

So that was how Linguini and I became a team. He said I could stay at his apartment. In the morning, we'd go back to Gusteau's and try to re-create the soup.

Linguini showed me into his apartment.

It was a little shabbier than most human places I'd seen. But it had a refrigerator and a hot plate! So I got up early the next morning and made breakfast. I think Linguini was a little surprised. He had thought I would run away. But working at Gusteau's was important to me. I wanted to start my first day off right!

Later that morning, we went to Gusteau's. I bet I made restaurant history as the first-ever rat chef. I was pretty nervous. Who knew what would happen if I was discovered! Not to mention it was pretty dark and stuffy under Linguini's shirt. But still, I had made it to Gusteau's, and I was ready to cook.

Chef Skinner—that was the mean chef's name—walked up to Linguini. "Re-create the soup," he said darkly.

So we started cooking. Actually, Linguini started cooking. If he reached for the wrong spice, I bit his hand. When he didn't notice he had dropped the spice tin into the soup, I bit his other hand. It drove him nuts.

I've always said that there are no cooking mistakes, just cooking adventures! It's not "the wrong spice," it's "experimental flavor"!

Linguini ducked into the food safe, where no one could see us. "This is not going to work, Little Chef!" he said. "We have to figure out something that doesn't involve any biting."

Just then, Skinner opened the door to the food safe. He looked shocked—as if he had seen me. But Linguini hit the lights, and I scrambled under his hat.

When Skinner turned the lights back on, Linguini played the whole thing off. I was safe for now. . . .

Chapter 5

When Linguini and I went back to the kitchen, we almost collided with waiter who was carrying a tower of dishes. Instinctively, I tugged on Linguini's hair. He bent over backward and practically limbo-danced under the waiter's tray! Maybe this was it—a way for us to communicate. Back at the apartment, we discovered that I could get Linguini to move in different ways by tugging his hair!

We spent a lot of time figuring it out. I blindfolded Linguini to get him to focus on the hair-pulling. If I pulled one way, he'd chop; another way, he'd crack an egg.

It was perfect! Hidden under his hat, I could control Linguini's movements almost as well as if they were my own.

The next day, we finished the soup.

"You will need to know more than soup if you are to survive in my kitchen, boy. Colette will be responsible for teaching you how we do things here," Skinner said. He pointed to the cook who had saved Linguini's job, and left.

Linguini turned to Colette. "I just want you to know how honored I am to be studying under such a—"

Colette stabbed a knife through his shirt-sleeve, pinning it to a table. "I have worked too hard for too long to get here, and I'm not going to jeopardize it for some garbage boy who got lucky. Got it?"

I felt Linguini's head nodding under me. Colette yanked the knife out of his sleeve. Then she turned and walked away.

Colette was tough, all right.

You always knew what she thought . . . about our chopping, for instance. "You waste energy and time!" she shouted, grabbing the knife to show us how it was done.

But Colette knew her stuff. She taught us that a chef keeps his arms close to his body and that good bread sounds crackly when you squeeze it.

Soon the customers started asking for a new dish from Linguini. See, the food critic had raved about my soup in the newspaper.

So Chef Skinner gave Linguini another challenge: Sweetbread à la Gusteau! "Colette will help you," Skinner added.

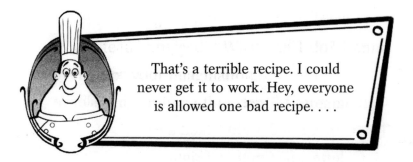

That's a terrible recipe. I could never get it to work. Hey, everyone is allowed one bad recipe. . . .

Colette, Linguini, and I got to work. Colette read the ingredients from the recipe card: anchovy-licorice sauce, dried white fungus, dog rose puree.

I didn't see how this was going to taste good. Then I had a crazy thought. Why follow the recipe? I steered Linguini around the kitchen to gather new ingredients. We began to make a different sauce.

Colette looked up from the sweetbread. "This is no time to experiment!" she cried.

"You're right," I heard Linguini say. Suddenly, he swatted at his hat—at me! *I* was the reason he'd been cooking so well, and now he didn't want to listen? I yanked his hair, and his hand slapped his face.

Colette eyed him warily, then set the dish on the counter for the waiter. "I forgot to add the anchovy-licorice sauce!" she exclaimed.

This was my chance. When Colette returned with her sauce, I made Linguini block her hand.

I could tell it was killing him, but I knew that the dish would be unbelievable with my sauce. I made Linguini pour it over the sweetbread.

Colette looked at Linguini angrily as the waiter, Mustafa, whisked the plate away to the dining room.

I didn't care that she was mad. All I cared about was what the customers thought.

It seemed like forever before Mustafa came back. "They love it!" he cried. "Other diners are already asking about it."

Inside Linguini's hat, I felt like dancing. I had created something completely new. And people liked it!

The rest of the evening was a blur. Everyone was ordering the new dish. Linguini and I made sweetbread all night. I had never worked so hard. I had never felt more like myself.

Chapter 6

After the dinner rush, I went outside. As I was standing there, enjoying the moment, I heard something rustling behind the trash cans.

"Remy!" a familiar voice exclaimed.

It couldn't be. Could it? "Emile?" I asked hopefully. I was so happy. I'd thought I'd never see my brother again!

"You're alive!" said Emile. "We figured you didn't survive the rapids!"

I hadn't thought they'd survived! Then my brother did something he'd always done: nibbled on some trash. *Blech!* There was no way I was going to let him eat that when I worked at the best restaurant in town.

While Emile waited outside, I scurried through the empty kitchen to the food safe. That was when I felt a pang of guilt.

"You are stealing?" my imaginary Gusteau said, appearing beside me.

"It's for my brother," I said. "It's just this once. . . ." Linguini would understand, wouldn't he? After all, I was helping him and the restaurant.

I ignored the nagging feeling of guilt and took some food out to my brother.

It did feel good watching Emile eat well for once. But I think he'd have been just as happy eating garbage.

"Hey!" Emile cried. "Dad doesn't know you're alive yet. We've got to go to the colony! Everyone will be thrilled."

Why wasn't I jumping at the chance to see everyone again? For so long, I had wished for nothing else. What had changed?

"Thing is," I said, "I kind of have to . . ."

Emile looked angrier than I'd ever seen him. He didn't understand how I could possibly choose anything over my family.

"It wouldn't hurt to visit. . . . ," I said.

"My son has returned!" my father cheered, raising my paw into the air. Emile had brought me to the sewer, where the rat colony had settled. Everyone was so excited to see me they threw me a party. A rat band played jazz while Dad, Emile, and I talked.

It was great to see Dad again. The commons were amazing—for a sewer. Dad told me it had been hard for them, moving and getting settled again. I felt bad about that. I was the one who had snuck into the cottage kitchen. If it hadn't been for me, we'd all still have been there.

"The important thing is you're home, Remy," said Dad.

Was I home? It was fantastic to see everyone again, but ever since I'd gotten there, I'd felt restless. I kept wondering what was happening at the restaurant.

"Well, uh, about that . . . ," I said. "I've found a nice spot not far away. I'll be able to visit often."

"You're not staying?" Dad asked, shocked.

How could I make this better? "You didn't think I was going to stay forever, did you?" I asked. "Eventually a bird's got to leave the nest."

Dad stared at me. "We're not birds; we're rats," he said.

I wanted him to understand that I wasn't one of them—I was different. "Rats," I began.

"All we do is take. I'm tired of taking. I want to make things."

"You're talking like a human," Dad said.

"Who are not as bad as you say," I responded. "I've, uh, been able to, uh, observe them at a close-ish sort of range."

My dad stared at me again. This was not going well. "Come with me," he said. "There's something I want you to see."

A few minutes later, Dad and I arrived at a shop. There were rattraps in the window—tons of them. "Take a good, long look, Remy. The world we live in belongs to the enemy. We're all we've got."

But I knew he was wrong. Look at how well Linguini and I were getting along. I explained that I thought I could change things. Then I began to walk back to the restaurant. I hated to leave, but I had to go. I had to be me.

Chapter 7

It took me until dawn to walk back to the restaurant. When I got there, Linguini was asleep on the floor. I found out later he'd been up all night with Skinner. The chef had tried to find out how Linguini had become such an amazing cook.

I heard a motorcycle pull up outside. Colette! I jumped onto Linguini's head and grabbed two fistfuls of his hair. I managed to get him up onto his feet. But he was still asleep! I steered him over to a pair of sunglasses and got him to put them on. Then I made Linguini chop vegetables.

A moment later, Colette came in. "So," she said to Linguini. "The chef. What did he say?"

When Linguini didn't answer, Colette got mad. "I see how it is," she said. "You get me to teach you a few kitchen tricks to dazzle the boss, and then you blow past me?"

I jumped on Linguini's head as hard as I could. He was still out cold.

Colette was getting more and more annoyed. "I thought you were different," she said.

Then the worst possible thing happened: Linguini started to snore.

Colette gasped, completely insulted, and slapped Linguini across the face. He spun around twice before hitting the floor. His hat went flying with me still hidden inside.

At least now he was awake.

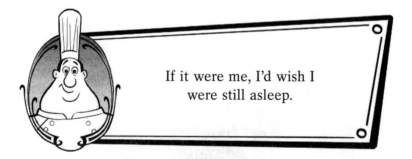

If it were me, I'd wish I were still asleep.

"I didn't have to help you," Colette yelled, holding back tears. "But I *wanted* you to succeed. I . . . *liked* you. My mistake."

"Colette! Wait . . . ," Linguini called as she stormed out. Then he turned to me. "It's over, Little Chef. I can't do it anymore."

Linguini put me and his hat back on his head and ran to Colette. "I have a secret," he told her. "I have this . . . this tiny . . . a tiny chef who tells me what to do."

"A . . . 'tiny chef'?" said Colette.

"Yes," Linguini replied. He pointed to his hat. "He's up here—"

"In your brain?" Colette said.

I couldn't let Linguini spill the beans! If Colette found out, I'd be kicked out of the kitchen.

The rest all happened so fast. Linguini started to lift his hat. I had to do something! I yanked on Linguini's hair. His head jerked forward and—he was kissing Colette!

It was a crazy thing to do. But I was desperate. Besides, neither of them seemed to mind.

Ah, yes. Love was in the air. They were young. They were in Paris. It was so romantic.

It was *soooooo* annoying.

Linguini was distracted whenever Colette was around. Sometimes he ignored me. Other times he took her advice instead of mine!

One night, Linguini took off with Colette on her motorbike and left his hat on . . . with me still under it!

When we took a sharp turn, Linguini dropped his arms to steady himself. The hat and I went flying!

I landed in the middle of a busy street. Cars whizzed by, just missing me.

Linguini and Colette kept going. Linguini was having so much fun, I don't think he even noticed.

When I got to the sidewalk, a woman in an outdoor café saw me.

"Rat!" she screamed. I ducked into a storm drain. I was out of danger.

"Disgusting little creatures," I heard someone say.

My heart sank. So that was how the world still saw me. It didn't matter that I could outcook most of them. What mattered to just about everybody was one thing: I was still a rat.

Chapter 8

Early the next morning, I arrived at Gusteau's. Emile and some other rats were waiting, and they looked hungry.

I couldn't believe that Emile had told the others about the restaurant. But I couldn't turn them away.

I told the rats to wait. Then I snuck into the empty kitchen and went to the food safe. It was locked. I looked over at Skinner's office. The key had to be in there somewhere. I was nervous, but no one was around. So I went in.

I scampered onto Skinner's desk. I was face to face with a picture of Gusteau. "Remy," it said, "what are you doing in here?"

I told Gusteau that I didn't like it, either, but I had to feed Emile and his friends. "If I can't keep them quiet, the entire colony's going to be after me," I said.

Then I spotted the key. It was under a file labeled *Gusteau: Last Will & Testament*. "Hey, your will," I said to Gusteau. Curious, I pulled out the file. Inside, along with the will, was an open envelope—with Linguini's name on it.

"Why would something about Linguini be filed with your will?" I asked Gusteau.

I guess I was being pretty nosy. But I had already come this far, so what did it matter?

Now, I'm a pretty good reader for a rat. But at first, this letter didn't seem to make any sense. Maybe that was because what it said about Linguini was so surprising.

"He's your son?" I said to the Gusteau portrait.

"I have a son?" Gusteau said, shocked.

"How could you not know this?" I asked.

"I am a figment of your imagination!" he replied. I kept forgetting that part.

My head spun while I thought about what I had discovered.

Did Linguini know? This would change his life. The will said he was the rightful owner of Gusteau's!

At that very moment, Skinner walked in. He saw me and froze, stunned.

I snatched the will and the letter and bolted. Skinner snapped out of it and began to chase me. He seemed desperate to get the papers back. That was how I knew he didn't want

Linguini to find out that Gusteau was his dad. He must have been trying to keep it a secret so he could have the restaurant! And a man with a secret can be a dangerous man.

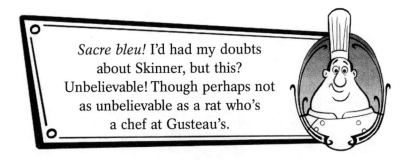

Sacre bleu! I'd had my doubts about Skinner, but this? Unbelievable! Though perhaps not as unbelievable as a rat who's a chef at Gusteau's.

I raced into the street. Skinner followed on his moped. I looked back and saw his cold eyes following my every move. There was no way he was going to let me escape. He caught up to me and tried to snatch the papers.

I came to a sudden stop, and he went zooming by, down some stairs. He landed in a heap at the bottom.

Relief washed over me. Then a bus roared by, and the gust of wind from it blew the papers

toward the river. I ran after them again, and Skinner hopped back onto the moped. He reached for the papers, but at the last second, I leapt up and got them!

I landed on a boat. From the riverbank, Skinner jumped aboard. I hopped onto the deck of another boat. Skinner followed! He chased me from one boat to another.

Then my luck seemed to run out. The next boat looked too far away. But I had to try. Using the papers as wings, I flew over the water and landed safely on the other boat.

Skinner knew this was it—his last chance to keep the restaurant. So he jumped, too. *Splash!* He plunged into the river. I saw him coughing and sputtering as I hopped up onto a bridge and ran off with the papers.

Chapter 9

Within the hour, I had found Linguini and shown him everything. The truth was out! Gusteau's belonged to him. The news even made the papers!

Now and then, Emile and his friends came by for food. I felt bad about taking from Linguini's restaurant. But I couldn't say no to my brother, either.

Linguini was too busy to notice. Sometimes he was even too busy to work! One evening, he was being interviewed by reporters in the dining room.

I sat and waited underneath his hat while he

chatted and posed for photos until well after opening time. When were we going to start cooking? Then he started talking about how Colette was his inspiration, like I'd had nothing to do with his success. I was so mad.

Just then, Anton Ego, the restaurant critic who had taken away one of Gusteau's stars, burst in. He announced that he would return for dinner the next night—and that Linguini had better be ready.

When Linguini and I returned to the office, I was still pretty mad. I guess it showed.

"Don't give me that look," he said. "Your opinion isn't the only one that matters. Colette knows how to cook, too."

Didn't Linguini realize everything I'd done for him? Without me, where would he have been? Not running his own restaurant, that was for sure! I yanked on his hair.

But Linguini didn't see it that way. He took me out back and told me to cool off. "Ego is coming and I need to focus," he said. "It's time you figured out who's in charge around here!" He stormed back into the kitchen.

Mon Dieu! Our little Remy has no idea that Chef Skinner is watching from the roof! Now Skinner knows that Remy is the secret chef!

I was so angry! I kicked some cans. Then I froze.

Emile and some other rats were standing there. They had heard what Linguini had said.

I realized that even if I was a good chef, no human was ever going to see past the fact that I was a rat. Dad had been right. It was time to look out for myself, for my own kind. I told them to come back later with everyone.

After the restaurant closed, I led the colony into the kitchen and opened the food safe. They were raiding the shelves when I heard a voice.

"Little Chef?" It was Linguini. I went to the door of the food safe. All around us, rats stood frozen to their spots.

"Look," Linguini said, "I don't want to fight. I've been under a lot of, you know, pressure." He sounded like the old Linguini now, the one I had wanted to help after he'd let me out of the jar. "The only reason anyone expects anything from me now is because of you," he said.

"I haven't been fair to you," he went on.

It was the worst possible time for him to find out that I was stealing from him. But that was exactly what happened. Inside the food safe, Emile was busy eating grapes. Reaching for one, he tumbled off a shelf and landed on his stomach. A small cheese wheel fell on top of him, and the grapes flew out of his mouth and hit Linguini.

Linguini looked inside the food safe and saw all the rats. "You're stealing from me?" he yelled. "How could you? I thought you were my friend. I *trusted* you!"

I tried to explain, to apologize. But Linguini was too angry to listen.

"Get out!" he screamed, and shooed us away. "And don't come back or I'll treat you the way restaurants are supposed to treat pests!" He slammed the door.

Standing there with my colony, I couldn't blame Linguini for being mad. I *had* been stealing from him. But had he meant it when he'd called me a pest? Did he see me the way the rest of the human world did?

Chapter 10

"Just can't leave it alone, can you?" Emile said behind me.

I was peeking through the kitchen window. Ego was coming to review the restaurant that night. Emile was right. I had to know what was going on in there. I had to know how Linguini was doing without me.

"You really shouldn't be here during restaurant hours. It's not safe," I told him.

"I'm hungry," Emile said. Then he began to look around for food scraps. He lifted a tarp and found a piece of cheese underneath. Emile didn't notice that it was sitting in a rattrap!

"No, wait!" I shouted. I knocked Emile out of the way just in time. But I fell into the cage myself!

Emile panicked. "I'll go get Dad," he cried.

All of a sudden, someone was looming over us. It was Skinner!

Emile hid as Skinner picked up the cage and carried me to his car. "You will create for me a new line of Chef Skinner frozen foods, and I, in return, will not kill you," Skinner said, putting the trap in his trunk.

I gasped. *Kill* me? What had I ever done to him?

"Au revoir . . . rat!" Skinner said.

With that, he slammed the trunk shut. In the darkness, I shook the bars of the cage. But it was no use.

Skinner seemed to have planned to get me out of the way so that Linguini would get a bad review from Ego. But how did he even know I existed?

Let's just say our little Remy was not as good at staying hidden as he'd thought, eh?

I guess it didn't matter. Now it was official: Linguini was on his own.

"So . . . we have given up," said my imaginary Gusteau, appearing beside me. "We are in a cage. Inside a car trunk. Awaiting a future in frozen food products."

"No," I snapped, "*I'm* the one in a cage. I've given up. You are free."

"I am only as free as you imagine me to be," Gusteau replied.

"Oh, please," I said, annoyed. "I'm sick of pretending. I pretend to be a rat for my father. I pretend to be a human through Linguini. I pretend you exist so I have someone to talk to. You only tell me stuff I already know. I know who I am! Why do I need you to tell me? Why do I need to pretend?"

Gusteau smiled kindly. "Oh, but you don't, Remy," he said as he faded away. "You don't."

And with that, imaginary Gusteau was gone. That was the last time I saw him. I guess I didn't need him anymore.

Chapter 11

Soon after that, I heard a crash. The car shook as a stone gargoyle came crashing right through the trunk. The next thing I knew, Emile was climbing in to rescue me! And he wasn't alone! After he'd seen Skinner lock me in the trunk, he'd hurried off to get Dad.

Working together, we opened the latch on the cage. I was free! I jumped out and hugged Dad and Emile. "I love you guys," I said, and hurried off.

"Where are you going?" Dad called after me.

"To the restaurant!" I called back. Being trapped by Skinner had helped me figure out a few things. One of them was that I really wanted to help Linguini . . . if he'd let me.

I was done sneaking into Gusteau's. I decided to walk into the kitchen through the back door, the way all the other chefs did.

Dad and Emile tried to stop me as I neared the door. But my mind was made up. I was tired of hiding and pretending. I was going to be me, even if people didn't like it. Like Gusteau had said, I had to be fearless if I wanted to be great!

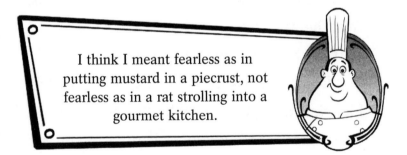

I think I meant fearless as in putting mustard in a piecrust, not fearless as in a rat strolling into a gourmet kitchen.

As soon as I went in, the cooks came at me. Every rat instinct I had told me to run for my life. But I knew I couldn't—or I'd always wonder what might have happened.

"Don't touch him!" Linguini shouted. "I know this sounds insane, but, well, the truth sounds insane sometimes." He paused for a moment, then took a deep breath. "The truth is I have no talent at all. But this rat . . . he's the one behind these recipes—the real cook."

Now everyone looked confused. I guess Linguini figured they needed to see us in action. So he lifted me onto his head. I tugged at his hair and steered his hand toward some spices. Then I made him lift them up so I could sniff them.

The chefs watched silently.

"Look, this works. It's crazy, but it works," Linguini reassured the cooks. "Together we can be the greatest restaurant in Paris. And this rat, this brilliant little chef, can lead us there. What do you say? You with me?"

I was touched by Linguini's confidence in me. Whatever the others thought, at least he was on my side.

No one spoke. No one moved. This was it: the moment of truth.

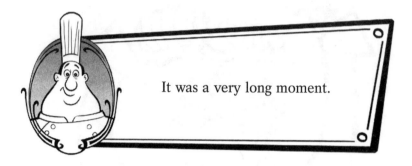

It was a very long moment.

One by one, the chefs all quit—even Colette, who looked mad and sad at the same time. I guess she was hurt that Linguini hadn't told her about me.

Linguini and I were the only ones left. Linguini peeked out into the dining room. The customers were getting restless. Ego was waiting for his food. Linguini turned, went to his office, and closed the door.

Chapter 12

I was alone. I had walked in and laid it all on the line. But I was still a rat. If no one wanted to work with me, what did it matter? I couldn't run a restaurant on my own.

That was when Dad stepped out of the shadows. I guess he'd heard everything. "I was wrong about you. About him." He gestured toward Linguini's office. "I couldn't do what you just did. I'm proud of you."

I was blown away by Dad's words. I had never thought I could be myself around him.

Dad let out a whistle, and the rest of the colony came out from their hiding places.

"We're not cooks," Dad said, "but you tell us what to do and we'll get it done."

At that moment, the back door creaked open. A man with a clipboard stepped inside and stared at the kitchen full of rats.

It turned out he was the health inspector. Slowly, the inspector backed toward the door— then turned and ran! I winced. If he got away, Gusteau's would be shut down before the end of the night!

"Stop that health inspector!" I shouted.

Dad and half the colony took off after the inspector. I looked around at the other half. I wasn't sure we could pull it off. But I knew we were going to try.

First things first: I needed to get these rats cleaned up. You couldn't be dirty and work in a kitchen. I herded them into the dishwasher for a quick shower. As they came out, I shouted their assignments.

"Team three will be handling fish!" I called.

"Team four: roasted items! Team five: grill! Team six: sauces! Let's go, go, go!"

Just then, Linguini came out of his office. He stopped and stared. Rats had taken over his kitchen.

His eyes lit up. "We need someone to wait tables," he said.

Immediately, Linguini put his roller skates on and skated around the dining room, passing out menus, water, and bread.

In the kitchen, my team was cooking up a storm. It was all I could do to keep a handle on everything. "Whoa!" I called to the salad team. "Compose the salad like you were painting a picture!"

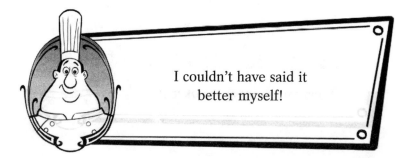

I couldn't have said it better myself!

We made dishes as quickly as Linguini could pick them up. He had just rolled into the kitchen to pick up an armload when the back door opened.

It was Colette!

"Oh, Colette," said Linguini, "you came back! Colette, I—"

She held up a finger, silencing him. "If I think about this, I might change my mind. Just tell me what the rat wants to cook."

I showed Colette the recipe I wanted her to make for Ego: Gusteau's Ratatouille, a simple stew of eggplant and other vegetables. She looked doubtful. We only had one chance to impress him.

"This dish is humble," she said. "Ego is not. Are you sure you want to serve this?"

I nodded. She shrugged and got to work.

The back door swung open. Dad and his team carried the health inspector in and brought him to the food safe.

I didn't want to think about how much trouble we were in. We had to focus on finishing Ego's dish. Colette was about to add the last ingredients, but I stopped her. I had an idea for a new-and-improved recipe. I pointed at some ingredients I'd collected.

"You want me to put those in instead?" she asked me. I nodded. Colette looked at me and shook her head. But I think I saw her smile a little, too.

In a flash, the dish was done. Linguini rolled into the kitchen, picked it up, and whisked it out to the dining room . . . to Ego.

Minutes later, Skinner burst into the kitchen from the dining room. He'd been waiting there secretly, sure that Ego would be disappointed.

"Who cooked the ratatouille?" Skinner shouted. "I demand to know!"

Dad's team overtook Skinner and put him in the food safe with the health inspector.

Meanwhile, in the dining room, Ego was complimenting Linguini on the ratatouille. I wish I could have been there to hear it. Linguini told Ego he had not made the ratatouille. Intrigued, Ego asked to meet the mystery chef.

We waited until all the other diners had left the restaurant. Then Linguini and Colette took me out to meet Ego. He smiled, thinking it was a joke. There was no way the chef could be a rat.

My heart sank, heavy with disappointment. *Forget it*, I thought. *He'll never take me seriously.*

As Linguini told Ego the whole story, Ego's smile faded.

When Linguini was done, Ego stood up and thanked us for the meal. Without another word, he left.

Chapter 13

I realized that no matter what Ego wrote, I was happy. It had been the best night of my life.

I didn't go home—not to the sewer or to Linguini's. I knew I wouldn't be able to sleep. Instead, I sat looking over the city, wondering what Ego would have to say.

The next morning, the colony and I met Linguini and Colette at Gusteau's to read the review in the newspaper.

I can't remember exactly what it said, but I think somewhere in there he called me the genius now cooking at Gusteau's. Oh, and the finest chef in France.

He said it without giving away my little secret. You know, my *species*.

Too bad we couldn't count on everyone to keep a secret. See, we had to let Skinner and the health inspector loose. Of course, they ratted us out. The Ministry of Health shut the restaurant down immediately. And, well, that was the end of Gusteau's.

The end of Gusteau's. The end of an era. But somehow, I think not the end of Remy's cooking career. . . .

After everything died down, Linguini, Colette, and I opened our own little bistro. It's not a five-star restaurant. It's just a cute little place that serves really good food. It even has a special spot for my friends and family to eat.

Colette and I handle the kitchen. Linguini handles the dining room. He makes sure there's always a table for Ego, our best customer and one of our investors.

If you're ever in Paris, you should stop by. We serve the best ratatouille you've ever had, I promise.